Flying Friends

Tales from Whispery Wood

Make friends with the animals of Whispery Wood!

Be sure to read:
Mole's Useful Day

... and lots, lots more!

Flying Friends

Julia Jarman
illustrated by Guy Parker-Rees

SCHOLASTIC

To Sam and Theo – J.J.

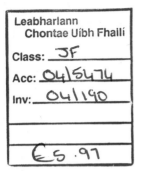

Scholastic Children's Books,
Commonwealth House, 1-19 New Oxford Street,
London, WC1A 1NU, UK
a division of Scholastic Ltd
London ~ New York ~ Toronto ~ Sydney ~ Auckland
Mexico City ~ New Delhi ~ Hong Kong

First published by Scholastic Ltd, 2002

Text copyright © Julia Jarman, 2002
Illustrations copyright © Guy Parker-Rees, 2002

ISBN 0 439 99454 3

Printed and bound by Oriental Press, Dubai, UAE

10 9 8 7 6 5 4 3

The rights of Julia Jarman and Guy Parker-Rees to be identified as the author and
illustrator of this work respectively have been asserted by them in accordance with the
Copyright, Designs and Patents Act, 1988.

Chapter One

It was evening in Whispery Wood.
Rabbit and Squirrel were under the old
oak tree listening to the wind whispering.

"Owl's got a new
friend," said Squirrel.

"That's nice," said Rabbit.

"No it isn't," said Squirrel.
"Owl doesn't like us any more.
He's got a flying friend. Look."

Rabbit looked up through
the branches of the old oak
tree. He saw the moon
in the darkening sky,
and Owl, swooping
and swirling!

"I can see Owl!"
cried Rabbit.
"Swooping
and swirling!
But he's all by
himself. I can't
see his new friend."

"That's because he can make himself
invisible," said Squirrel.

"Invisible!" cried Rabbit. "That's exciting!"

"No it isn't," said Squirrel.
"It's strange."

"Oh!" cried Rabbit.
"There's his new friend now! What sort of
creature is he?"

"Don't know," said Squirrel. "He's a bit
like a bird, and a bit like a rat, and he's got
ever such a squeaky voice."

Owl's new friend wasn't a bird or a rat.
He was a long-eared bat, and
Owl loved flying
with him.

He did aeroBATics!

He looped the
loop and swooped
and swirled at
supersonic
speeds.

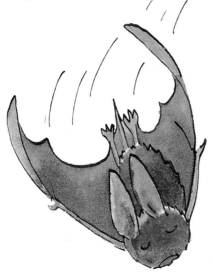

His squeaky voice
echoed through
the wood.

"I think they're playing Hide and Squeak," said Rabbit. "Look!"

But Squirrel didn't want to watch Owl playing with his new friend. HE wanted to play with Owl.

"Owl likes his new friend more than me – or you," he said.

Rabbit shook his head.
"Oh no, Squirrel.
Owl has lots of
friends and he
likes us all. I'm
his Under the
Tree friend.
You're his In
the Tree friend.

Now he has an Above the Tree friend too.
Look, he's coming down to see us."

Owl landed on a
branch. Bat flew down
to join him.

"Good evening, Rabbit!" he hooted.
"Good evening, Squirrel! Come up and
meet our new friend,
Long-eared Bat!"

Bat was swinging from the branch, upside down. He waved cheerily and squeaked,

I'm a bat, not a rat
A long-eared bat
With leathery wings
And fur like a cat!

Rabbit laughed. "I think he heard you, Squirrel."

But Squirrel wasn't listening.

Bat did a somersault.

I'm quicker than a bird
Nimbler than a gnat
I'm a long-eared leathery-winged
AcroBAT!

"Acrobat! That's good!" Rabbit laughed
and clapped. "Welcome to Whispery
Wood, Bat!"

"Do come up,
Squirrel!" Owl
hooted. "Come and
do acrobatics with Bat."

"Go on!" said Rabbit.
"I'll watch. It will be
good fun."

But Squirrel still wasn't listening. He was feeling jealous. "I'm Owl's In the Tree friend," he muttered. "He doesn't need a new friend."

Owl flew down. "Don't be shy, Squirrel. Bat is longing to meet you. We're going to have such fun together. Bat is going to live with us in the old oak tree."

"Sorry," said Squirrel, bounding off.
"Can't stop. I've got to see Mole."

"See you tomorrow night then!" Owl
called after him. Then he flew up to Bat.
"Come on! Let's have another game!"

Rabbit watched as the flying friends took
off into the starry night.

Chapter Two

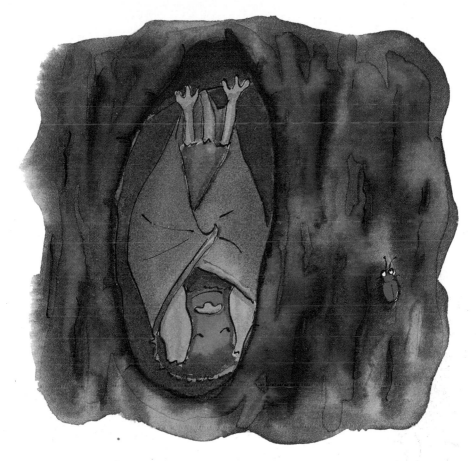

Bat loved his new home in Whispery
Wood. During the day he slept in the old
oak tree, with his long leathery ears tucked
under his wings.

But at night he and Owl gave flying
displays!

The other animals clapped and cheered.
All except Squirrel.

Bat whizzed so fast you could hardly
see him, but he never bumped into things.
Owl loved flying with him.

But one
night when
Owl woke up
Bat didn't
come out
to play.

"Wakey, wakey, Bat!" Owl hooted loudly.
"The moon's up. Let's go flying!"
But Bat didn't answer and he didn't
come out.

Owl flew into the old oak tree to look for him. Bat was hanging upside down as usual.

"Wakey, wakey!" Owl lifted one of Bat's long ears. "Rise and shine!"

Bat opened one eye, but he wasn't his usual cheery self.

"Oh dear," said Owl, "whatever is the matter, Bat? Are you poorly?"

At first Bat didn't answer. Then he squeaked, "N-nobody likes me."

Owl couldn't believe his feathery ears. "Nobody likes you? But we all like you!" he said. "You've seen everyone clapping and cheering."

Bat shook his head.
"They used to, but they
don't now. Now they just
call me names."

"Names? What names?"
said Owl sternly.
Bat didn't answer.

"I'm sure you are mistaken,"
said Owl. "Come on. Let's fly
around for a bit. Let's do
some loop the loops.
Everyone will come
out and watch.
You'll see."

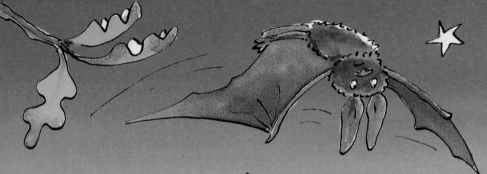

Owl and Bat flew round Whispery Wood, looping the loop, but no one came out to watch. No one clapped and cheered, and when Owl swooped low he could hear the animals whispering.

Bloodsucker!

Quick!
Hide! There goes
Bumper Car!

Big Ears!
Big Ears!

Squeaker!
Squeaker!

Sticky Bun!

"See?" said Bat,
as the two friends
flew back to the
old oak tree.

"They don't mean it,"
said Owl. "They're
only joking. Come on.
Let's go visiting.
There's Rabbit.
Let's drop in on
him first. He's
very kind."

"Good evening, Rabbit!" said Owl.

"Good evening, Owl," said Rabbit.

"How nice to see you."

Then he saw Bat and hopped into his burrow. "Got to go! You're with Sticky Bun. He might stick in my fur."

"Stick in your fur!" laughed Owl. "Bat isn't sticky!"

Bat smiled and squeaked,

I'm a bat, not a bun
I can be lots of fun.

"Feel his furry face," said Owl. "Feel his long leathery ears!"

Rabbit looked as if he wanted to. He put out a paw, but then he pulled it in again.

Owl peered into Rabbit's burrow.

"Is there someone with you, Rabbit?"

Rabbit didn't answer and Bat looked sad again.

"I think you're being very unkind," said Owl. "Come on, Bat, we'll go and visit Mole instead."

Mole was looking out of a molehill,
sniffing the air with her big pink snout.
Suddenly she shouted, "Hide everybody!
I can smell Bloodsucker!"

And she dived into her hill.

Owl found her. "You're being very silly,"
he said. "Long-eared bats
don't suck blood.
Vampire bats
suck blood."

"Don't take any notice of her," he said,
turning to Bat, but Bat had gone.

"Bat! Come back!" Owl hooted, but there
was no reply.

Chapter Three

Owl looked for Bat all over Whispery
Wood, but he couldn't find him anywhere.
Bat didn't come home to the old oak tree
and in the middle of the night there was
a terrible storm. Owl was very sad. He
thought he would never see Bat again.

Next day he
called a meeting.

By twelve o'clock most of the animals
had arrived.

Mole sniffed the air with her big pink snout. "Good! I can't smell Bat," she said. "We must have frightened him away. I called him Bloodsucker!"

"And I called him Big Ears!" said Hedgehog.

IMPORTANT
MEETING
Midday
Old oak
tree
Owl

Owl hooted, "Stop it!
This is exactly why I've
called the meeting!
To talk about Bat.
You've all been
very cruel."

The animals stopped their chatter and Owl looked at them sternly.

"Bat was my friend," said Owl. "He wanted to be your friend too, but you hurt his feelings and he has flown away. How could you be so cruel?"

Owl was right. Bat had decided to leave
Whispery Wood for ever. But as he was
flying over the northern edge, something
stopped him. His long ears began to
vibrate. Someone was crying for help!

Back at the meeting, none of the other animals heard the cry. Even Owl couldn't hear it. He was still talking about his friend.

"Why didn't you try to understand him? His long ears were useful. He could hear sounds we can't hear. His squeaky voice was useful too. It's a supersonic squeak which helps him find things."

Owl was right about that too. Bat's long ears heard Squirrel crying for help! Bat's supersonic squeak let him know where Squirrel was – miles away on the other side of Whispery Wood.

The other animals hadn't even noticed Squirrel was missing.

Owl looked at them crossly. "Who started this name-calling?" he asked.

They all looked at their feet.

Nobody answered. "He isn't here, is he?" said Owl. "It's Squirrel, isn't it?"

Rabbit's voice quavered. "H-he thought you liked B-bat more than you l-liked us."

Owl nodded, "So he said bad things? Silly Squirrel. Silly, bad Squirrel. And now we shall never see poor Bat again."

 Chapter Four

Suddenly, they heard a squeaking sound
up above them.

"Owl!" cried Rabbit. "It's Bat! Oh, Bat,
I'm so sorry. We're all very sorry."

But Bat squeaked, "Later! Listen."

The animals listened hard, but all they heard was the wind whispering through the trees.

"Can't you hear Squirrel crying for help?" said Bat. "He's trapped in Hazel Copse on the south side of Whispery Wood."

"But that's miles away," said Rabbit.

"There's no time
to waste," said Bat.
"He needs help fast.
His tail is trapped."

"I'll go and tell him help is
coming," said Owl. "Get
Badger if you can."
"No, I'll go. I'm faster
than you," said Bat.

Then Bat whizzed off, squeaking his
supersonic squeak all the way!
"Don't worry, Squirrel.
Help is coming!"

Bat flew without stopping to the other side of Whispery Wood.

There was Squirrel, in Hazel Copse, with his tail trapped under a huge log.

"B-bat!" he gasped. "B-but…"

"Don't say a thing," Bat squeaked. "Help is on the way."

Soon the other animals arrived. Owl took
charge.

"One. Two. Three. Heave!" said Owl,
and together they heaved the log off
Squirrel's tail.

"Thank you," said Squirrel later.
"Especially you, Bat. You heard my cry for
help with your long ears. You comforted me
with your squeaky voice. You flew to the
rescue with your leathery wings. I want to
say I'm sorry, from the bottom of my heart."

"I'm sorry," said Mole, "from the bottom of my big pink snout."

"I'm sorry," said Hedgehog, "from the bottom of my prickly ickly, er … bottom."

"Sorry Bat," said Rabbit, "from the…"

But Bat had gone.

High above, they could hear his squeaky voice!

I'm a bat! I'm a bat!
I'm a long-eared bat!
Quicker than a fox
Nimbler than a gnat!
I'm a high speed aerobatic,
acro-bat!

"Who's for a game of Hide and Squeak with our friend Bat?" said Owl.